Evelyn in Purgatory

Topher Payne

SAMUEL FRENCH

FOUNDED 1830

SAMUELFRENCH.COM
SAMUELFRENCH-LONDON.CO.UK

FOR PRODUCTION ENQUIRIES

UNITED STATES AND CANADA
Info@SamuelFrench.com
1-866-598-8449

UNITED KINGDOM AND EUROPE
Plays@SamuelFrench-London.co.uk
020-7255-4302

Each title is subject to availability from Samuel French, depending upon
country of performance. Please be aware that EVELYN IN PURGATORY
may not be licensed by Samuel French in your territory. Professional
and amateur producers should contact the nearest Samuel French
office or licensing partner to verify availability.

MUSIC USE NOTE

Licensees are solely responsible for obtaining formal written permission from copyright owners to use copyrighted music in the performance of this play and are strongly cautioned to do so. If no such permission is obtained by the licensee, then the licensee must use only original music that the licensee owns and controls. Licensees are solely responsible and liable for all music clearances and shall indemnify the copyright owners of the play(s) and their licensing agent, Samuel French, against any costs, expenses, losses and liabilities arising from the use of music by licensees. Please contact the appropriate music licensing authority in your territory for the rights to any incidental music.

IMPORTANT BILLING AND CREDIT REQUIREMENTS

If you have obtained performance rights to this title, please refer to your licensing agreement for important billing and credit requirements.

EVELYN IN PURGATORY was originally produced by The Essential Theatre Company (Peter Hardy, Artistic Director) on July 5, 2012 at Actor's Express in Atlanta, Georgia. It was directed by Betty Hart, with sets was by Reed Higgins, costumes by Jane Kroessig, sound by Jon Summers; lights by Harley Gould, and props by Kathy Manning. The Stage Manager was Anna Pages, with production management by Jennifer Kimball. The cast was as follows:

CANDACE METZGER. . . . . Megan Hayes

LILA WADKINS . . . . Jo Howarth

EVELYN REID . . . . Amanda Cucher

TOBY FLEMING. . . . . Jonathan Wierenga

FRED DISALVO. . . . . .Rial Elsworth

ROBERTA BURKE . . . . Betty Mitchell

ATWOOD. . . . . .Josie Burgin-Lawson

CHARACTERS

CANDACE METZGER – 30s. The person with the most power in the room, and the least qualifications for it. From New Jersey, tries to hide the accent but fails when she gets emotional.

EVELYN REID – 30s. Likeable and resourceful. A careful mix of guarded pleasantry – she has a stellar game face. New England native.

LILA WADKINS – 50s. Calm, maternal, thoughtful, witty. The voice of reason. The art teacher everyone wishes they had. Upstate New York native, some residual hippie around the edges.

TOBY FLEMING – 20s. A bit of a geek. Quiet, passive-aggressive, perpetually uncertain. Brooklyn native.

FRED DISALVO – 50s. Bombastic, funny, a bit of a bully. A gym teacher from Hell's Kitchen, back when that still meant something.

ROBERTA BURKE – 60s. The self-appointed queen of all she surveys. Razor-sharp wit, no patience, and an uncanny ability to spot the weaknesses in those around her. Very Bronx.

ATWOOD – *(unseen)* The head of the disciplinary panel. The invisible voice of absolute authority. Written as "Ms. Atwood," but can be changed to "Mr. Atwood" to accommodate a gender swap.

SETTING

A windowless, forgotten office deep in the Department of Education building, New York City.

TIME

Autumn 2008 through Spring 2009.

*In memory of Jo Howarth, who always knew
we'd get this play published.
Look at that, Jo. We did it.*

ACT ONE

Scene One

(SETTING: A windowless, forgotten office in the Department of Education building in Manhattan. The carpet is stained, and the room could use a fresh coat of paint. There is a desk and filing cabinet by the room's single door, which leads to the hall. A telephone and a late model desktop computer are on the desk. There are four chairs and an artificial plant nearby, a coat rack, and absolutely nothing else. The time is Autumn, 2008.)

(DISCOVERED AT RISE: **CANDACE METZGER** *is seated at the desk, sorting a large stack of papers. She is in her early thirties, dressed in comfortable office attire.* **LILA WADKINS** *enters, carrying a large canvas tote bag. She is in her fifties, with a cheerful disposition and natural warmth. She wears a peasant blouse and skirt, crafty jewelry. She signs her name on a clipboard at the desk, prompting a nod of acknowledgement from* **CANDACE**. **LILA** *sits in one of the chairs, pulls a small knitting project from her bag, and commences knitting. The phone rings.* **CANDACE** *answers.)*

CANDACE. Metzger, 704. *(She jots a quick note.)* Thank you.

(She hangs up and continues sorting papers. **EVELYN REID** *enters. She is a well-dressed woman in her thirties, wearing a suit and heels, carrying a briefcase. She takes in the room a moment, then approaches the desk.)*

1

EVELYN. Excuse me.

CANDACE. Yes.

EVELYN. Evelyn Reid, James Madison High School.

CANDACE. Yes.

EVELYN. I was told to find a room to wait in…will any room do?

CANDACE. Yes.

EVELYN. Could I wait here?

CANDACE. Sign in, please.

EVELYN. Alright. *(She does.)* Will I be reassigned to another classroom today, or tomorrow?

CANDACE. It's different for everyone.

        (**LILA** *chuckles.*)

EVELYN. I'm sorry, it's just, I'm not really clear on how this works. All they told me was to come here instead of my school. Do you know what time my hearing will be?

CANDACE. Miss Reid –

EVELYN. Mrs.

CANDACE. *Mrs.* Reid, I am just the proctor for the room, I have no information on individual cases. The way this works is, you sign in and take a seat. When it is time for your hearing, they will call. Until it is time for your hearing, you wait. You will do this every day. Have a seat, please.

EVELYN. Alright. *(starts for a chair, stops)* What do you mean every day?

CANDACE. Mrs. Reid. Please just take a seat.

        (**EVELYN** *walks to a chair and sits.*)

LILA. You don't want to sit there.

EVELYN. I'm sorry?

LILA. That's Fred's chair.

EVELYN. Is Fred here?

LILA. No, but he will be soon. And that's his chair. He's very protective of his chair.

EVELYN. Alright.

(She gets up and moves to the next seat.)

LILA. That one's taken as well, I'm afraid.

EVELYN. You're joking.

LILA. That would be Roberta's chair. You do not want to take Roberta's chair.

EVELYN. You are aware that none of these people are in the room?

LILA. Please do not sit there. If Roberta comes in and finds you in her chair we will all suffer. She's worse than Fred.

EVELYN. I suppose the chair next to you is –

LILA. Toby's. We lost a teacher last Thursday. Since then everyone's had a chair. If you insist on sitting, take Toby's. He won't put up a fight.

EVELYN. I'll stand.

LILA. Oh, it's fine, people always take Toby's chair. He just stakes out a spot over in the corner. He's young, his joints can take it. Come sit.

EVELYN. *(standing)* I'm fine, really. I'm sure it won't be that long.

LILA. Dear. We've been here long enough to claim chairs. Long enough to have a very intricate hierarchy of chair ownership. Trust me, it will be that long.

EVELYN. Are you all awaiting reassignment?

LILA. We are waiting for our hearings. No one is reassigned. Not ever. You will have a hearing, eventually, where they present and discuss the charge against you. From there you either return to your classroom, or you're sent packing.

EVELYN. How long does it take to get a hearing?

LILA. It's different for everyone. Toby's been waiting about three weeks now.

EVELYN. He's come here every day for three weeks? My god.

LILA. Yes. Fred calls him "Rookie." But perhaps that auspicious title will go to you now. Roberta has been here since just after Labor Day, so that's roughly, what? Seven weeks? Fred and I are both holdovers from last school year. I got here in March, Fred was…January? January.

EVELYN. January? He's been waiting for a hearing for ten months?

LILA. Roughly.

EVELYN. But that's insane! Why on earth would they keep anyone waiting that long?

LILA. Mrs. Reid, is it?

EVELYN. Yes. Evelyn.

LILA. Lila Wadkins. Art teacher at Joseph P. Benson. Formerly. Now I'm just the occupant of this chair. Evelyn, there are over a million students served by New York public schools. Seventy thousand teachers. If any of those teachers are accused of impropriety, they are sent here until the case can be reviewed in a hearing. That process takes time. It's a measure put in place to protect the students, and also to allow the teacher due process.

EVELYN. You're defending this?

LILA. The concept, yes. If the teacher is guilty, it protects the students from being placed in a potentially toxic environment. And the innocent teachers are given the opportunity to defend themselves. So much time is wasted, however. But you'll still collect your paycheck, so there's no need to worry.

EVELYN. But I didn't do anything wrong! I'm innocent!

LILA. The claim of every man in prison. Nothing can be done, Evelyn. Might as well stake out this chair now or try to find a room with an unclaimed seat. But brace yourself. At any given time there's several hundred teachers in this building, and every room is its own little fiefdom. I've seen fist fights. So unless you've got a good right hook, I'd grab Toby's chair and take advantage of his lack of backbone.

(**EVELYN** *hesitates, then sits.*)

EVELYN. Isn't there anyone you can talk to, at least to get an update?

LILA. Of course. Candace? Do you have an update on when my hearing might be?

CANDACE. I'm just the proctor, Mrs. Wadkins. I have no information on individual cases.

LILA. Thank you dear.

CANDACE. Sure thing.

LILA. And there you have it.

EVELYN. That's it?

LILA. Yes. That would be it. Everything I've shared with you came from other teachers. There's no official communication whatsoever.

EVELYN. But my students –

LILA. Are in the care of a marginally qualified substitute. Do not go back to your campus. Do not communicate with other instructors or students at your school. Both are grounds for immediate termination and loss of your teaching certificate.

EVELYN. It's like prison for teachers.

LILA. No. It's like purgatory for teachers. Welcome to the rubber room, Evelyn.

(**LILA** *returns to her knitting.* **EVELYN** *pulls her cell phone from her purse and holds it up, trying to get a signal.*)

EVELYN. Damn it.

LILA. You won't get a signal in here. I think it's all the lead paint.

(**EVELYN** *stands.*)

I wouldn't get out of that chair.

(**EVELYN** *sits.*)

EVELYN. *(To* **CANDACE**.*)* Excuse me. May I use your phone?

CANDACE. No personal calls, Mrs. Reid.

> *(***TOBY FLEMING** *enters, carrying a backpack. He's in his late twenties, youthful and a bit socially awkward. He wears jeans, a polo shirt, and a jacket. He's listening to an iPod Shuffle, clipped to his shirt. He signs in and heads for the chair occupied by* **EVELYN**. *He stops and stares.)*

EVELYN. I'm sorry, I –

> *(***LILA** *puts a hand on* **EVELYN**'s *shoulder.)*

LILA. Good morning, Toby. This is Evelyn. It's her first day.

> *(***TOBY** *lets out a disgusted sigh, then looks at the other two empty chairs. He heads for the corner and begins setting up his laptop computer.)*

EVELYN. Oh, he looks mad.

LILA. He's fine. Really. He's used to it. Did you say you teach at Madison High?

EVELYN. Yes. American history.

LILA. Is Elena Vargas still your guidance counselor?

EVELYN. Yeah. You know Mrs. Vargas?

LILA. She was at Benson, before they laid her off and gave us one counselor for five schools. Now our kids are only allowed to have problems on Thursdays. I was a reference when she interviewed at Madison. I haven't spoken with Elena in years.

TOBY. You know, we agreed on Thursday we weren't going to take on anyone new. I'm just saying.

LILA. Toby, this is not a clubhouse. People can come and go as they wish.

EVELYN. I'm sorry. You can have the chair. I'll take the floor.

TOBY. No no no, it's fine. I'm fine. I'm just saying we agreed after Harold left, is all. There was an agreement.

LILA. I agreed to nothing, Toby dear. I sat here knitting.

CANDACE. The time is now eight a.m.

(**CANDACE** *takes the clipboard off her desk and replaces it with another holding a red piece of paper. She picks up the phone and dials.*)

EVELYN. She doesn't do that every hour, does she?

LILA. It means the day has begun.

EVELYN. What do we…do?

LILA. Exactly what we were doing. Nothing. But Fred and Roberta are now officially late to do nothing. I have a trashy magazine if you'd like.

(**LILA** *pulls a tabloid from her tote bag and hands it to* **EVELYN**.)

CANDACE. Metzger. 704. Wadkins, Lila. Reid, Evelyn. Fleming, Toby.

FRED. (*Offstage.*) Don't hang up! Don't hang up!

(*She hangs up.* **FRED DISALVO** *rushes in. He's a paunchy man in his 50s, wearing a sweatshirt, khakis, and sneakers. He looks at the red sheet on the desk.*)

Oh come on, lady, gimme a freakin' break! One minute late! I was waiting for the elevator! Call me in! Tell 'em you missed my name!

CANDACE. I can't do that. I don't make the rules, Mr. Disalvo.

FRED. Yeah, so what do you care if we bend 'em a little? One minute! Come on!

CANDACE. Sign in, please.

(**ROBERTA BURKE** *enters. She's in her 60s, dressed very conservatively. A bit of a spinster, but intentionally so. She glowers at the clipboard.*)

ROBERTA. You've already called in, haven't you?

CANDACE. As my job requires me to do every day at eight, Mrs. Burke.

FRED. One freakin' stupid minute. Come on!

ROBERTA. Ya get a sick little thrill out of having them dock our checks, don't ya? You sadist.

FRED. The buses go as fast as they go, lady. We don't control it.

ROBERTA. I am an old woman. What, I run up the stairs, I slip, I break a hip? Is that what you want? A poor defenseless old woman lying at the bottom of the stairs, moaning in agony.

CANDACE. I'm just doing my job, Mrs. Burke.

ROBERTA. Look, O'Brien –

CANDACE. My name is Metzger. Candace Metzger.

ROBERTA. Read *1984*. You're O'Brien in the flesh. Now break free of Big Brother and give me the damn white clipboard, you fascist.

> (**CANDACE** *does not move.*)

FRED. Oh, come on! We don't do anything here! Why the hell does it matter? I'm not signing it.

ROBERTA. We refuse. We protest.

CANDACE. If you don't sign in on the tardy sheet, you will be marked as absent from the reassignment center for the day. Three unapproved absences will result in immediate termination.

FRED. Oh for god's sake...

> (**FRED** *signs in.* **ROBERTA** *signs in. They both turn to face the room, focusing on* **EVELYN**.)

ROBERTA. I thought we had an agreement.

TOBY. Thank you.

LILA. Roberta, honestly.

FRED. We said after the black guy left we weren't taking on any more strays.

TOBY. His name was Harold, Coach. Not "The Black Guy." Why would you even point that out?

FRED. I was just describing the guy.

ROBERTA. There are other rooms. Many other rooms. This place is a hive.

EVELYN. Perhaps I should go.

> *(She takes her briefcase and stands.* **TOBY** *jumps up.)*

LILA. If you go to another room you have to sign in as tardy. They cut your pay when you're tardy. Toby, sit.

> *(***TOBY*** *sits.)*

Evelyn can stay with us for the morning, and find another room after lunch if she wishes. And as for you two, nobody took your chairs, so I fail to see how it's of any real concern to either of you. Everyone, just take your seats.

> *(***FRED*** *and* ***ROBERTA*** *sit.* ***FRED*** *takes a folded piece of cardboard taped under his chair, produces a deck of cards, and begins playing Solitaire. Meanwhile,* ***ROBERTA*** *digs through her tote bag and pulls a plastic sign reading "JANITORIAL." She goes to the door.)*

CANDACE. What are you doing?

ROBERTA. I pulled it off a door downstairs. This way nobody else will come in.

CANDACE. Mrs. Burke, you cannot do that.

ROBERTA. What's the problem here? The janitor already knows where his closet is. He doesn't need signage.

CANDACE. Mrs. Burke, if you put the sign up, I will remove it.

ROBERTA. And then I will put it back up again. We could fill the whole morning with that little game.

CANDACE. No.

FRED. Oh, come on!

ROBERTA. Show me, in writing, the rule against labeling rooms as janitor's supply closets, and I will put this away.

CANDACE. I am certain there is a rule against it.

ROBERTA. Well. You let me know when you find it. *(She attaches the sign and slams the door.)* Sure wish I'd thought of this yesterday.

TOBY. So. Evelyn. What're you in for?

LILA. You don't have to answer that.

ROBERTA. Yes she does.

EVELYN. It's all a horrible mistake. I'd prefer not discussing it, if it's alright.

ROBERTA. If you don't tell us, I will make something up and report it as fact. I don't get a lot of entertainment around here.

TOBY. She will. She'll make something up. None of the Puerto Rican teachers will talk to me. They won't say why, but I know it was her.

FRED. I'll tell ya why I'm here. Because the whole school system's gone straight to hell.

TOBY. Really, Fred? I thought it was because you broke a kid's wrist.

FRED. Shut up. See, these two Hell's Kitchen punks gang up on a sissy kid in the hall –

TOBY. Hell's Kitchen punks? When does this story take place, 1960?

FRED. Shut up, you'll get your turn.

TOBY. It's not exactly "West Side Story" over there anymore. Most of it's gone condo. I'm just sayin'.

FRED. There's still people there from the old neighborhood. And their kids are punks. So they grab this scrawny kid, start beatin' the crap outta him. I step in, try to stop it. They fight me, I fight back. What, I'm supposed to take that? Let some little jackass take a swing at me? So I knock his ass on the ground, he breaks his wrist. Here I am. Almost a year now. The kid's still in school. Not even freakin' detention for him. Twenty years ago, hell, ten years ago, I woulda been doin' my job. Now I'm some kinda criminal. The whole system's gone straight to hell.

(**CANDACE** *rises quickly and exits. They all watch, and* **EVELYN** *looks back for explanation.*)

TOBY. We don't know where she goes. She just does that sometimes.

LILA. They want to cut art classes at my school. Something must be eliminated, and somehow we have reached a point where fostering creative expression is no longer a necessity. But my students are artists. They win awards. National. They go on to Pratt, DePaul, Parsons. You can't cut funding from a program producing those kinds of results.

EVELYN. That's wonderful.

LILA. The principal, a former football coach with whom I have exchanged no end of unpleasantries, claimed I was being insubordinate. Hostile. Which is absurd. In the seventies I lived in a communal household with fourteen people, I know how to be a team player. But the accusation was all it took. I was sent here, and now my program is dying.

ROBERTA. It's a holocaust.

LILA. I will remain here until I have no job to go back to, and then I will be dismissed.

EVELYN. I'm so sorry.

LILA. I just ache for my students. They won't all be athletes or math scholars. Some of them are meant to be artists. They just need an instructor who trusts them, believes in them. And we're taking that chance away. It breaks my heart.

ROBERTA. It didn't used to be such a gee dee battle. You're on your own out there. Not worth it.

TOBY. Roberta is here by choice.

EVELYN. Beg your pardon?

ROBERTA. I kept seeing teachers being sent here for months on end, collecting a check, not having to put up with the hoochie coochie show we now laughingly call public schools. And there I was, retirement just within reach, trying to sell Shakespeare to gang bangers when I could be sitting on my duff with a good book. Sign me up, sounds like a sweet deal to me.

EVELYN. So what did you do?

FRED. This is great.

ROBERTA. You know the little monsters who wear their pants saggy, underwear on full display?

EVELYN. Yes. Yes I do.

ROBERTA. I had this one in particular. I've intentionally forgotten his name. If it wasn't his pants, he was sleeping in class, backtalk, or texting. One glorious Thursday, I asked him to come to the board and list the major characters in "Pride and Prejudice." In his childlike hand, he scrawled Stewie, Meg, Peter, Quagmire –

TOBY. From *Family Guy*, the cartoon.

EVELYN. Right.

ROBERTA. So I pantsed him.

(**FRED** *bursts into laughter.*)

EVELYN. What?

ROBERTA. I grabbed his fully-exposed red boxer shorts, and I pantsed the little bastard! Let him display his pockmarked tookus to the whole class. He'd been figuratively showing his ass since September, the literalism was pure heaven. The next day I grabbed a copy of "Mansfield Park" and came here.

EVELYN. My god! Roberta, that's horrible!

ROBERTA. Oh, don't lie. It's fabulous. I had forty years of teaching on my side. It was obviously a momentary lapse brought on by stress. I was contrite in my hearing. They understood.

EVELYN. I'm confused. You've already had your hearing?

FRED. She's had three.

ROBERTA. I haven't spent more than six weeks in a classroom in the last two years. I wasn't nearly as poetic with the other offenses. For the best, really. How could I top the first time?

TOBY. Sequels never live up to the original.

ROBERTA. A few well-chosen profanities in front of the Catholics will get you out of there pretty quick. If my next hearing doesn't happen until spring, I can retire without ever going back.

LILA. You should be in your classroom, Roberta. Your students need you. It's such a waste.

ROBERTA. They don't need me. They need someone who still cares. I keep suffering momentary lapses brought on by stress.

(**ROBERTA** *pulls a book from her bag.*)

EVELYN. What about you, Toby? Why are you here?

TOBY. I suffered a momentary lapse brought on by stress.

LILA. Toby's lapse was genuine.

TOBY. I just… I thought it would be different.

LILA. First year teaching.

EVELYN. Ohh.

(**CANDACE** *returns and goes to her desk.*)

FRED. That break wasn't authorized, lady. Didn't ask permission.

ROBERTA. Better sign the red sheet.

CANDACE. *(Fuming.)* I have different rules.

(**CANDACE** *dials the phone.*)

EVELYN. What do you teach, Toby?

TOBY. Earth Science and Chemistry. I love science. I had terrible teachers when I was a kid, but I still loved it. And I always thought if I could get in a classroom, show them why it's awesome, what makes it spectacular, I could inspire them. But I didn't. I couldn't.

CANDACE. *(Into phone.)* Metzger. 704. Tardy report. Disalvo, Fred. Bite my – *(She stops, glares at* **ROBERTA**.*)* Burke, Roberta. *(She hangs up.)* This is an official document, Mrs. Burke. Your use of profanities will be on the record and could affect the outcome of your hearing.

ROBERTA. You wanna mess with me, missy? Show me what ya got. Let's dance.

(**CANDACE** *ignores her.*)

EVELYN. You were saying, Toby?

TOBY. It was just this maze of bureaucracy and pointless crap, and the administrators had this hive brain like the Borg, I was always getting stonewalled and shot down, they don't want you to innovate, just get them ready for testing. One day, my kids were supposed to be doing this stupid essential skills test that means absolutely nothing, and they just wouldn't shut up –

FRED. He started crying. Like a girl.

TOBY. Shut up, Fred.

FRED. He cried and threw a globe.

LILA. The first year is hard on every instructor.

FRED. Picked up the whole world and hurled it.

ROBERTA. Very metaphorical. Atlas throws a tantrum.

FRED. How'd you pitch it, Toby? Underhanded or over your head?

TOBY. Fred, I've got a pretty good feeling you're not missed at your school.

FRED. Hey, Rookie. It's coaches like me who kept Hell's Kitchen boys from busting your skull in high school. Now they send us to the rubber room. Who's gonna keep sissies like you alive?

TOBY. I'm not a sissy, Fred. I'm a geek. There is a difference.

FRED. Drama Club, A/V Club, same thing. Not one of you can throw a damn ball.

TOBY. My principal's doing what she can to, you know, speed things along. So we'll see. It'll get better when I go back. You just gotta deal with the disappointment, I guess.

ROBERTA. No, Toby. The situation doesn't change. Your expectations do. Evelyn, your turn.

LILA. It's not her turn. This isn't group therapy.

EVELYN. No, it's only fair. Um. Well. Natalie Clark, one of my seniors. In my class for the second time. I've tried working with her, but nothing changes. She doesn't care. Six weeks in, she's already failing. I told her last week if she doesn't change course it's likely she won't graduate. Natalie threw a fit. Said I'm against her, have it out for her. Then yesterday she told the principal she saw me in my classroom, kissing the captain of the track team.

TOBY. Oh crap.

ROBERTA. Was it true?

EVELYN. Absolutely not! It's absurd. Anyone who knows me would say so. The girl's a liar.

FRED. Could happen. Athletes mature faster.

TOBY. No they don't.

FRED. How would you know?

EVELYN. I am married. Happily. And I would never – I denied it. Vehemently. And the boy denied it. But my principal says they still have to investigate, hold a hearing. What is there to investigate when everyone involved says it didn't happen?

LILA. They'll talk to your students, your colleagues, see if anyone else saw you behaving inappropriately with the boy.

TOBY. Maybe you'll get to see the shrink. That's a load of laughs.

EVELYN. This is humiliating.

LILA. This is due process.

FRED. This is a load of crap.

LILA. Evelyn, I hope your situation is resolved quickly.

FRED. It won't be, but you go ahead and hope.

ROBERTA. There is nothing more dangerous than a child who lies. Nothing. They can destroy entire institutions. And this generation? god help us. The children feed on this culture of victims like ciphers. Like living in "The Crucible."

TOBY. We did that play. My junior year. First show they did after we put in the new sound system, and then they barely had any cues.

ROBERTA. That's what you remember from "The Crucible." The absence of musical numbers.

TOBY. Not musical numbers. I could've done ambient noise, environmental sounds. Set a mood.

FRED. We were supposed to read that in school. I didn't.

ROBERTA. Then how did you pass English?

FRED. I was the quarterback.

LILA. Not every problem is new.

ROBERTA. You missed out on one of the greatest dramatizations of American hysteria ever written. Back me up on this, Lila.

LILA. Actually I've never read it either.

ROBERTA. Evelyn?

EVELYN. I saw "Death of a Salesman."

ROBERTA. Well that's not the same damn thing, is it?

EVELYN. It's Arthur Miller.

ROBERTA. Oh for god's sake. It should be required reading.

TOBY. It is. We just didn't do it.

(**FRED** *laughs.*)

ROBERTA. Oh, forget it.

EVELYN. We could read it here. I mean, we've got all this time on our hands, why not put it to good use? It'd be like a book club.

FRED. Yeah, ah, I'm not gonna do that.

EVELYN. Well, participation isn't compulsory. But the rest of us, we could meet maybe twice a week. Hopefully we'll all be gone before we're done with the play.

LILA. god bless your sweet naiveté. Oh, why not? We could use an activity. Safeguard our brains against atrophy. Toby, you'll do it too.

TOBY. Why do I have to if Fred doesn't?

LILA. Because there's still hope for you.

ROBERTA. Alright. I'll go to Barnes and Noble tonight. But
you should know, I have impossibly high standards.

EVELYN. Don't worry, Roberta. We'll keep our pants up.

(Lights fade.)

Scene Two

(Three weeks later. **ROBERTA**, **EVELYN**, *and* **LILA**
have pulled their chairs together. **TOBY** *sits at their*
feet. Each is holding copies of The Crucible,
except for **LILA**, *who is knitting a nearly-completed*
sweater. **FRED** *is playing Solitaire.* **CANDACE** *is at*
the desk, typing.)

EVELYN. My point is, John still believes that his reputation,
and the lack of any evidence, will exonerate him. He
believes in the system. All he's asking for is fairness.

LILA. But he shouldn't expect fairness. Not from them.
There's a reason they call it a witch hunt.

ROBERTA. The temptation to abuse absolute power is too
tasty. Why, just look at Candace.

*(**CANDACE** shoots her a look.)*

Give her a telephone and a clipboard, she thinks she's
Margaret Thatcher. But you never see it as abusive if
you agree with them. It's only an abuse of power in the
eyes of the dissenter.

TOBY. Okay, okay, I get all that, but at some point you gotta
look around and see the world you're living in, and
find a way to survive. It's basic human instinct. Survival.
Proctor could have just signed the damn paper, said
he's a warlock, and skipped town with Liz. Start over.

EVELYN. Because he has no control over what happens
after he gives in. If he just tells them what they want to
hear, it gives them all the power, because now they're
in charge. The mistake he makes is letting them put
him on the defensive.

LILA. Well, wouldn't you be in his position?

EVELYN. The counsel has no evidence, and John knows it.
He doesn't have to prove he isn't a witch. They have to
prove that he is.

LILA. Or he could simply remain silent. Why doesn't he
refuse to participate in their little game?

FRED. Because it's his name, people! Come on! It's all he has left! You're not testing integrity until you're doing it in hostile territory. Christ, do you people even get this guy at all? Even if he ditches town, he'll always know the name John Proctor is worthless someplace, and he won't sleep at night!

ROBERTA. Go on, Fred.

FRED. I've been listening to you hens cluck about this stupid play for weeks now, and you've been missing the simplest concept. Valuing honor, over saving your own skin. That's what character is, people.

ROBERTA. But when Elizabeth lies to cover for John's adultery, is that a show of strength or weakness in her own character?

FRED. She lies. She loses. Even though she didn't know it, if she'd just told the truth and said he'd banged that cuckoo Abigail chick, they woulda been home in time for supper. You lie, you lose. Every time.

EVELYN. I'm afraid history disagrees with that assessment, Fred.

FRED. History agrees. Watergate. Monica Lewinsky. You lie, you lose.

EVELYN. They didn't lose because they lied, they lost because they got caught. Plenty of people in power have lied to save their own skin. But when it works, nobody ever knows.

LILA. Is that what you tell your students?

EVELYN. I tell them if you want to make history, you need the strength of your convictions. As long as you win, you're celebrated.

LILA. And if you lose?

EVELYN. Then generally you're forgotten entirely. If the Revolutionary War had turned out differently, George Washington would be a historical footnote who was hanged as a traitor, and we'd all have British accents.

TOBY. And better TV shows. BBC America kicks ass.

(**CANDACE** *gets up in a hurry and runs out the door.*)

FRED. And there she goes.

TOBY. Where she stops, nobody knows.

ROBERTA. Fred, you've inspired such lively discussion.

EVELYN. Welcome to the book club.

FRED. I'm not in your damn club.

LILA. Well, you've obviously been paying attention.

FRED. *(Pulling his chair over.)* Bah. Not really. Though I'll tell ya somethin'. I knew a Mary Warren once. Ugly woman. No neck. My wife made our boy take piano from her for about a minute. He couldn't stand her. Said her house smelled like onions.

LILA. I didn't know you had a son.

FRED. Yeah. Freddie Junior. You, ah, you got kids, Lila?

LILA. Oh, yes. Two girls. Lynne works in an accounting office here in the city, and Maureen's a bank teller in Albany.

FRED. Neither of them went artsy-fartsy for ya?

LILA. I think being utterly conventional was their form of rebellion.

EVELYN. Wait. Seriously, you people have been in the same room, all this time, and you never talked about your families?

TOBY. You've been in here like three weeks, and you haven't brought it up either.

EVELYN. Well, yes, but we've talked about plenty of other things. Where we went to school, food allergies. I'm not criticizing, I'm just surprised. How about you, Roberta? Any kids?

ROBERTA. No. Wanted, but it didn't happen for us.

LILA. You could've adopted.

ROBERTA. Oh really, Lila? Adoption, you say? Wow, we never thought of that. Gordon had cancer. Twice. Nobody wanted to give us a baby, because of the risk of it coming back. As though perfectly healthy people don't get cancer after they have kids, but there you have it. So it was just us, and that was fine. Until the cancer did come back. So maybe those bastards were on to something after all. Someone else talk.

(**CANDACE** *returns and sits at the desk.*)

LILA. Toby? You don't have children, do you?

TOBY. No, but I want 'em. I mean, one day. Gotta find a wife first, but yeah. I love kids. I'd love a son. Or a daughter. But something about guys and sons, I guess. Be a Boy Scout leader, play catch.

FRED. Gotta learn how to throw a ball.

TOBY. Fred, I know how to throw a ball, I just derive no pleasure from doing it.

FRED. You are such a weirdo.

TOBY. Evelyn? Kids?

EVELYN. No. We want to wait until we're a little more settled. When the timing's right.

FRED. Timing's never right. Just gotta do it and figure it out. Kids are messy and pricey, no way around it. Just jump in.

ROBERTA. I agree. If you both know you want it, just start trying. You never know what's gonna happen.

EVELYN. Hey, Candace, you married?

(**CANDACE** *doesn't respond.*)

TOBY. Oh come on, Candace, we're having a nice moment here. Don't be a wet blanket.

LILA. Now, now. Candace has work to do.

TOBY. We were trying to include her.

ROBERTA. She's not married. No ring. I've checked.

FRED. Well, that answers the kid question.

(**CANDACE** *begins to sob.*)

LILA. *(rushing over)* Oh, no, now you've done it.

FRED. Done what? What'd I do?

LILA. Nothing. Just, nothing. Talk to each other.

ROBERTA. Why on Earth would we talk to each other when this is so much more compelling?

LILA. You hurt her feelings.

FRED. Oh, come on. Candace doesn't have feelings. Or she didn't until now, and who coulda planned for that?

LILA. Just hush, you Neanderthal. She's pregnant.

(**CANDACE** *looks up, stunned.*)

ROBERTA. You are not!

CANDACE. I – But what makes you think –

LILA. My dear. You stopped drinking coffee two months ago. And lately you've had worse morning sickness than I had with Maureen. You're what, second trimester?

CANDACE. Sixteen weeks.

LILA. Come over here, dear.

(*She pushes* **CANDACE** *in the rolling desk chair over to the group.*)

EVELYN. Well, congratulations, Candace. That's wonderful.

CANDACE. No, it isn't!

ROBERTA. Who's the father? Do you know the father?

LILA. Roberta, of course she knows the father.

CANDACE. Sort of.

FRED. What the hell does that mean?

ROBERTA. Were you drugged at a party?

EVELYN. Roberta.

ROBERTA. They call them roofies.

CANDACE. It was just this guy from my building, Noah? We got to talking at the mailboxes one day, and he mentioned he had the complete series of *Lost* on DVD, I'd never seen it because I don't have cable and I get bad reception on ABC, so he started bringing the DVDs over and we'd watch an episode or two and then we'd talk about it and then we'd have sex. I really got into it, *Lost* I mean, the sex was just okay, but it became like a little routine and I find routines very comforting, you know?

LILA. Yes. Routines are comforting.

CANDACE. Noah didn't use condoms because he said he had this latex allergy, which I never really believed but I was on the pill and I knew he was safe. He was one of those guys Jewish people hire to sit with their dead people, and he had cauliflower ears from wrestling in high school, it's not like he was some stud, who would sleep with that?

ROBERTA. Depends on what's on television, apparently.

CANDACE. I was on antibiotics because I'd had strep and I didn't know that made my pills stop working, and then he moved out a few weeks before I found out, and I didn't even know his last name, he was just Noah the dead people sitter who I slept with through six seasons of *Lost*, and then maybe four episodes of *Breaking Bad* but I just couldn't get into it, and oh my god why in the name of Christ am I still talking?!

> *(She breaks away, rolling her chair back to the desk. Everyone is without words.)*

TOBY. You should really give *Breaking Bad* another chance, it gets pretty awesome later on. *(Stares from the group.)* Well, fine. Someone else say something.

EVELYN. It's okay, Candace. Really. You know, Nelson Mandela was an unplanned pregnancy.

ROBERTA. Edgar Allen Poe.

LILA. So was Oprah, look how she turned out.

FRED. Jesus.

EVELYN. Thank you, Fred. Also Jesus. You're going to be just fine.

CANDACE. Of course. Thank you all for your concern. I apologize. I need to get back to work now.

LILA. Now, Candace, sweetheart –

CANDACE. I am still the proctor in this room, Mrs. Wadkins. I need to get back to work.

LILA. Of course.

> (**LILA** *walks back over to the group.* **CANDACE** *rises and starts to leave.*)

EVELYN. Oh, Candace, don't leave!

CANDACE. I have no choice! I gotta pee! Again!

> (*She exits.* **EVELYN** *goes to her briefcase and removes a folder. She sits and begins filling out forms.*)

FRED. Wow. If only she'd had cable.

LILA. Fred.

FRED. I'm sorry, but not even knowing the guy's last name?

TOBY. That is kinda sad. Not as sad as the poor S.O.B. having cauliflower ears. But it's sad.

FRED. A wrestler. At least he was an athlete.

TOBY. If rolling around with another guy in spandex makes you an athlete, there's some undiscovered talent in the West Village.

LILA. The father's out of the picture anyway, his extracurriculars are irrelevant.

ROBERTA. Well. It's done now. We have to help her.

LILA. Really?

ROBERTA. She's a gee dee wreck. The child won't survive its first night alone with her. So we will help. If there's anything public schoolteachers know how to deal with, it's unplanned pregnancies.

> (*Everyone concurs.*)

FRED. She needs to watch her diet. Exercise. There's vitamins she's gotta take.

ROBERTA. There you are, Fred. Make a plan for her. We should be writing this down.

> (**ROBERTA** *goes for her purse.*)

EVELYN. We could have P.E., every afternoon. Do it together.

TOBY. You really won't be satisfied until we have a full roster of activities in here, will you?

EVELYN. Nope.

(**ROBERTA** *pulls a cell phone from her purse.*)

ROBERTA. Whose phone is this?

FRED. Jesus, there it is. I've been looking for it since yesterday. What's it doing in your purse?

ROBERTA. Well apparently that's where I put it when I stole it. I'm old. I can't account for all of my actions.

FRED. My wife jumped down my throat for losing this damn thing.

ROBERTA. Do you need an apology? Because if it means that much to you, I can make that happen, but I'd be apologizing for something I don't remember doing, so it won't be all that sincere.

LILA. What are you working on, Evelyn?

EVELYN. The union finally mailed paperwork. I'm filing a formal complaint.

TOBY. About what?

EVELYN. About what? About this. The rubber room.

ROBERTA. You're wasting your time.

EVELYN. Maybe I am. But every day I'm not at my school is another day Natalie Clark's walking around saying whatever she likes. I'm trying to clear my name. I can't just sit here and do nothing.

TOBY. Just like John Proctor.

EVELYN. And in the meantime I will continue with the book club, and P.E. for Candace.

LILA. I could teach her to knit.

EVELYN. Fabulous, I can learn too.

TOBY. I'm not knitting. I don't have to. I want that acknowledged.

(**CANDACE** *returns. Everyone looks at her.*)

CANDACE. What?

ROBERTA. We're going to help you, missy.

CANDACE. I'm sorry?

ROBERTA. The father is off to points unknown, keeping corpses company. You need help preparing for this child.

CANDACE. I'm giving the baby up for adoption.

EVELYN. Oh. Well, that's wonderful.

ROBERTA. All the more reason to get to work. The manufacturer doesn't skimp on parts and labor just because they're not keeping it at the factory. Fred will be your personal trainer, Lila will teach you to knit booties. Evelyn and Toby's responsibilities will be assigned later.

EVELYN. I know French.

CANDACE. How does that help?

EVELYN. Just what I've got. I teach history. My options are limited.

LILA. Oh, that sounds like fun! Ooh-la-la! You know, we had a French-Canadian woman back at the collective. Genevive was her name. She spoke flawless English until you asked her to pitch in and wash a dish or something, and she'd go blank and say, "*Je suis désolé?*" I was not a fan of that woman.

TOBY. Remember when we used to just come in and do our own thing? That wasn't so bad. I had my own projects.

ROBERTA. You can do your own projects at home. This is our project now.

CANDACE. What's the catch?

LILA. There's no catch.

ROBERTA. Yeah there is. The tardy clipboard. You won't be needing it anymore.

CANDACE. Fine.

FRED. Oh man, this is a very good day.

*(The phone rings. **CANDACE** answers.)*

CANDACE. Metzger. 704. Yes? *(She looks at the group.)* Of course. Thank you. *(She hangs up.)* Change in plans. Mrs. Burke, it's time for your hearing.

> *(Immediately* **ROBERTA** *is caught in a single overhead light. All others depart. She is addressed by an unseen voice.)*

ATWOOD. Good afternoon, Mrs. Burke. My name is Ms. Atwood, these are my colleagues Mrs. Martinez, Mr. Chen, and Mr. Hughes. We appreciate you coming in. According to your file, this is your third suspension from your position as an English teacher at PS 482, Paul Robeson Complex, Bronx, is that correct?

ROBERTA. Yes, that is –

ATWOOD. Mrs. Burke, after forty years without incident or complaint, you have been suspended for a series of infractions in the last two years, most recently for using profanities in the presence of students. Do you care to explain?

ROBERTA. Yes, Ms. Atwood. In recent years I found myself unprepared for the change in attitudes of my students, as well as the shifting expectations of my own position as their instructor. I allowed my own frustration to lead to a series of unfortunate moments. I am confident that once I return to my classroom, the Department of Education will be pleased with my restored commitment to my students' subject aptitude, test scores, and overall well-being. I can only offer my most sincere apologies for my past lapses in judgment.

ATWOOD. Mrs. Burke, given your long-standing commitment to New York public schools, we are reinstating you in your position at PS 482. Return to your classroom as usual tomorrow morning. We wish you all the best. Let's keep a lid on the sailor talk, alright?

ROBERTA. Absolutely, Ms. Atwood. Thank you for your time.

> *(Blackout.)*

Scene Three

(One month later. A small Christmas tree is on **CANDACE***'s desk. Music in the style of Dean Martin plays.* * **LILA**, **TOBY**, *and* **CANDACE** *are all in workout clothes, lifting free weights.* **TOBY***'s are considerably heavier than the ladies'.* **FRED** *walks amongst them in a sweatsuit, wearing a whistle around his neck.)*

FRED. Nice and easy, Lila. Don't jerk those up, just a slow, fluid motion. Rushing it won't get you in shape any faster, and it only leads to injuries, ladies. Ya hear that, Toby?

TOBY. Bite me, Coach.

FRED. Atta boy, working out the spine a little too. Come on, just seven more. Candace, count us down.

LILA. In French!

CANDACE. *(As they continue to talk.) Sept, six, cinq, quatre, trois, deux, un!*

FRED. Lila, good form. You're getting some results there.

LILA. I just want to reach a point where parts of my body don't unexpectedly flap in a strong wind.

FRED. *(Blows his whistle.)* Ladies, rest. Toby, chest flies. Three sets of twelve.

> (**TOBY** *drops to the floor as* **FRED** *takes* **CANDACE***'s weights and the others set theirs down and drink water.* **FRED** *stops the music.)*

CANDACE. Time check.

LILA. I've got ten after one.

> (**CANDACE** *crosses to the phone and dials as* **EVELYN** *enters, holding a large folder.)*

EVELYN. I got it! I got my file!

---

*The publisher recommends that licensees create an original composition that stays true to the author's intent.

FRED. Your lawyer got 'em to release it?

EVELYN. With help from the union, yeah. Even if I don't know when my hearing is, at least I can prep for it.

LILA. Ooh, I've never seen one. Does it have your letters of support?

EVELYN. Bunches. I haven't been through it all yet. There's at least one for Natalie Clark, but it's from her minister, he'd have to say something nice.

TOBY. Oh god, I'm dying. I'm gonna drop these on my face.

FRED. Well, keep going until ya do.

CANDACE. Shhh! Bonjour. Afternoon report. Metzger. 704. No tardies, none absent. *A la prochaine. Bon apres-midi.*

(She hangs up.)

EVELYN. Your pronunciation's really improved, Candace.

CANDACE. I got a collection of Celine Dion's French albums on eBay.

LILA. Evelyn, what else is in the file?

EVELYN. It's mostly my annual evaluations, test scores –

FRED. Those stupid evaluations. Isn't it a laugh? We tell the kids stuff's goin' on their permanent record, but we're the ones who really have 'em.

EVELYN. Oh my god, Natalie Clark's mother wrote a letter supporting me.

FRED. Holy crap, there's your winner.

LILA. That's so sad. I mean, it's wonderful for you, but… wow.

FRED. Any letters against? I bet I got a few against me.

CANDACE. Oh, Fred, I'm sure no one wrote anything against you.

TOBY. I'm not so sure. You can only make a geek play dodgeball so many times before he composes a strongly-worded letter.

FRED. Quit stalling.

TOBY. I'm done. You're killing me. I need hydration.

FRED. Wimp.

TOBY. Nazi.

CANDACE. I'll bet Lila's kids wrote letters.

LILA. I don't care if they wrote letters, I just hope they kept up with their art. You know, my juniors from last year are applying to colleges. Their portfolios are due right after the new year to be considered at conservatories. I'm obsessing over that, when I should be thinking about what I'll do when I lose my job. I should quit now, find something.

CANDACE. Lila, if your position is eliminated, you could be a proctor. A brain-damaged housecat could be a proctor.

LILA. Thank you for the vote of confidence.

CANDACE. You know what I mean. It's just playing warden and entering old mimeographed school records into that dinosaur computer.

TOBY. Is that what you do?

CANDACE. I don't think my bosses even know what I do. Nobody checks.

LILA. Oh, everyone! While we're on a break, I have a little something for all of you.

> *(She reaches into her tote bag, and pulls out several wrapped packages.)*

FRED. Are those Christmas presents?

LILA. Might be. Let's see… Evelyn? Evelyn? You alright, dear?

EVELYN. What? I'm sorry. Got a little engrossed in reading.

LILA. This is for you.

EVELYN. Oh, Lila, you didn't have to get me anything.

LILA. *(Passing out gifts.)* I didn't *get* you anything. You all watched me sit here working on them for months, it shouldn't even be a surprise.

> *(The group opens their gifts, each producing a handmade sweater.)*

EVELYN. Oh, how lovely!

FRED. Well, get a load of this.

TOBY. You said you were knitting these for your daughters.

LILA. Well, I lied. My daughters told me they are completely stocked up on all knitted items for the rest of their lives. Candace, I made yours a little oversized, so you'll get enough use out of it. When you've returned to your usual size, just cut the back open and use it as a, oh, what do they call it? A Slanket?

TOBY. Or a Snuggie, yeah.

CANDACE. *(Hugging* LILA.*)* Oh, thank you, Lila! It's getting so hard to find anything to wear! I'm gonna go put it on!

> *(*CANDACE *grabs a gym bag.)*

FRED. Hey, Metzger. I haven't released you yet.

CANDACE. We're done, coach. Rushing won't get us in shape any faster, and will only lead to injuries.

> *(*FRED *blows his whistle.* CANDACE *exits.)*

LILA. Everyone put your sweaters on! I want to see if they fit!

EVELYN. Give me just a minute, let me just finish reading this.

LILA. Fred. Sweater.

> *(*TOBY *and* FRED *put their sweaters on as the conversation continues.)*

LILA. Oh, Toby, come here. Your sleeves are too long, aren't they? By the way, Fred. I must compliment your stellar instruction in our workout plans.

TOBY. Lila's right, Fred. I feel great. I mean, not right now. Right now I want to die. But in general.

LILA. Stand still, Toby.

FRED. It's kinda nice to man up for once, isn't it boy?

TOBY. And I no longer feel great. I just tried to be nice there, you all saw it.

FRED. Oh, come on, Toby. I'm just bustin' your balls.

TOBY. You acknowledge I have balls. That's good.

LILA. Boys. 'Tis the season to be jolly. Evelyn, he looks alright if I just cuff the sleeves like this, don't you think?

EVELYN. Lila, I just need one second, okay?

LILA. Maybe bell sleeves look a little feminine.

FRED. Then it's perfect.

TOBY. Fred!

FRED. Come on, Rookie. If you're going back into that classroom you gotta learn to man up. Grow a set.

TOBY. Fred, I like watching Stargate, not painting my toenails, okay? Why can't you just hold me to the Crucible model? I'm a hardworking man who understands the value of my name and reputation. Bam. I'm John Proctor. Without the hanging.

LILA. We should read another play. That was fun.

FRED. Fine. You're a nice kid, Toby. Forget about it.

TOBY. A nice kid. But not a man.

FRED. I didn't say that.

TOBY. Because I'm not tough.

FRED. You've never been challenged. You give up, you cry, you throw globes. You're the poster child for what happens to boys who don't play team sports. You're soft. You're weak.

LILA. *(singing)*
GOD REST YE MERRY GENTLEMEN, LET NOTHING YOU DISMAY...

TOBY. Lemme ask you something, Fred.

FRED. What?

TOBY. What sport does your son play?

FRED. What the hell does my son have to do with anything?

TOBY. Theory I'm working on. I know you had Freddie Junior in uniforms before he was outta diapers. What's his sport?

FRED. Freddie Junior did it all in high school, kid. Baseball, football, basketball, was on the golf team, tennis. Did hockey –

TOBY. And never found one he did well.

LILA. Stand still please.

FRED. He couldn't decide between them. Renaissance man.

TOBY. How 'bout college? He still in school? Play anything now?

FRED. Why don't you just quit with askin' me about my kid?

TOBY. Is he soft, Fred? The boy who bears your name? Is he weak?

LILA. This conversation is not in any way productive, and I –

TOBY. *(breaking away from her)* Not now, Lila.

FRED. Shut your trap about my son, Toby.

TOBY. See, I got this theory, you never liked those types, but you got stuck with one in your own house, and now it makes you freakin' nuts. You couldn't toughen up your own namesake. And every guy you meet like me reminds you that with the only one who mattered, you failed. Am I right?

FRED. You don't know shit about anything, you little prick.

TOBY. I think I'm right. I am dead on here. Does he even talk to you? Oh, shit! You got a gay kid, Fred?

LILA. Stop it, Toby. Evelyn, a little help?

EVELYN. *(reading)* Not now, Lila.

TOBY. It's okay, you guys. I'm just bustin' his balls, right Coach? You're still smarting over your kid not being the quarterback, or whatever your damn ESPN macho horse shit expectations were! You pull that crap with me, you do it to your students, and you probably still do it to your son. When is that game gonna be over, Coach? When are you gonna concede defeat? You wanna talk about being a real man, Fred? Try showing some respect.

FRED. *(seething)* You're done. We're done. Come tomorrow, you get yourself a new room. You're out. We are done here, do you understand me?

TOBY. You're not in charge here.

FRED. If I see you here tomorrow, I will break your goddamn nose. Try me. I will put you in the hospital. You got me?

> *(**CANDACE** enters, distraught. Her sweater looks more like a poncho.)*

CANDACE. Oh god, I look like Mama Cass!

LILA. Oh, it's my fault, I should have measured you.

CANDACE. No, Lila. It's a beautiful sweater, really.

LILA. No, dear, I overestimated everything. Look at Toby. His sleeves look like an Elizabethan costume.

CANDACE. It's not the sweater, it's me. I feel like somebody inflated me. I can't tie my shoes anymore. I could still do it this morning. I've actually gotten bigger *since this morning*!

TOBY. It's okay. I got your shoes, Candace.

> *(**CANDACE** sits. **TOBY** kneels, tying her shoes. **LILA** goes to **FRED**.)*

LILA. Fred Disalvo. Everyone in this room will be here tomorrow. End of discussion. You're too damn old to act like a bully.

> *(**LILA** grabs her tote bag, and dress from coat rack, and starts for the door. She stops at **EVELYN**. **FRED** watches in silence.)*

Evelyn, are you –

EVELYN. I'm fine, sorry, there's just so much information to process here. *Je suis désolé.* Go get changed. I'm gonna try on my sweater. I love the color so much!

> *(**LILA** exits as **EVELYN** folds a document and puts it in her purse, then puts on her sweater.)*

CANDACE. Is it ready?

TOBY. What?

CANDACE. The surprise! Is the surprise ready?

TOBY. Oh. Yeah. Right.

CANDACE. Bring it to my desk.

> (**TOBY** *grabs his laptop, sets it on the desk.*)

FRED. What's up with you? Find a letter against?

EVELYN. No. I'm trying on my sweater for Lila. Pay me no mind.

FRED. I get it. You're gonna take his side.

EVELYN. I barely heard the exchange. I'm not on anyone's side. Let me be. I'm not involved.

> (**TOBY** *goes to his bag, digging.*)

FRED. Well, there's a first. You're the one pushing us to open up, be buddy buddy in here, but you don't say one damn thing about yourself. You got talent. Kinda spooky.

EVELYN. All I want is to go back to my life, Fred.

CANDACE. *(Looking at the laptop screen.)* Toby, what is this?

TOBY. Nothing!

> *(He runs back to close the laptop.)*

CANDACE. Are you writing a screenplay, Toby?

TOBY. It's just a stupid thing I'm toying around with.

CANDACE. Can I read it?

TOBY. No!

CANDACE. What if it's good?

TOBY. What if it's not?

CANDACE. What's it about?

TOBY. I don't wanna talk about it.

CANDACE. Oh, come on, Toby. Please?

TOBY. This, um, astronaut. He was on a space station alone, and he went crazy, just from the loneliness, the monotony. And he's in Deep Space, they can't send him back to Earth, so they send him to this other space station with other astronauts who also, um –

CANDACE. Went space crazy?

TOBY. Yeah. And they're all awaiting mission reassignment. But then this evil alien queen recognizes their weakness and attacks, and they all go to this planet where the women have wings, and… It's totally stupid, I know.

CANDACE. I'd watch that.

TOBY. Yeah?

CANDACE. Totally! Wouldn't you, Evelyn?

EVELYN. Heck yeah I would.

(EVELYN *goes to the desk.*)

TOBY. *(Types and clicks.)* Here we go.

CANDACE. Evelyn, you're a genius.

EVELYN. Oh, Toby made it happen, I just had the idea.

(LILA *enters, dressed, with her gym bag.*)

CANDACE. Lila, you've got to come see this.

LILA. Did you get internet in here?

TOBY. Yeah, Candace snuck into an office upstairs and I set up a wireless router from their server.

LILA. "Yes," would've sufficed. I didn't understand anything after.

TOBY. Come sit. Look at this.

(LILA *sits at the desk as* FRED *goes to* EVELYN*'s purse and pulls the folded document. He goes to his chair and reads, covering it with a newspaper.*)

CANDACE. What do you see?

LILA. A painting.

EVELYN. Be more descriptive. Critique it.

LILA. Why?

CANDACE. Just play along.

LILA. Alright. A street scene. The use of color is good. It's hard to tell on the computer, but based on the blending and texture it looks like oil on masonite. The shapes aren't sharp enough for realism, but not off-kilter enough to be impressionistic, so there's room for growth in one direction or the other – whose painting is this?

TOBY. *(looking at screen)* Ricky Torrence.

LILA. From my school? Did he start a website?

EVELYN. No. We did.

CANDACE. Evelyn had your students scan their portfolios.

EVELYN. While we're not allowed to contact our own students, there's no rule against contacting each other's. And you were so worried about your seniors getting their projects together before the holidays. So Toby set up a site.

LILA. Oh, gosh, isn't this against the rules?

TOBY. You're nowhere near them. All you're doing is looking at a website.

EVELYN. You know they need you, Lila. It's not the best-case scenario, but you can teach. From a distance.

TOBY. And they recorded videos with questions, showing you their process, it's pretty great.

(He hands her a headset.)

Here, put this on.

LILA. *(to the group)* Thank you. Thank you so much. *(puts on headset)* I guess I've got work to do.

*(**TOBY** and **CANDACE** watch **LILA**. **EVELYN** goes to her chair and spies her purse, open. She goes to **FRED**, who folds the newspaper on his lap.)*

EVELYN. Give it back.

FRED. What's that?

EVELYN. You stole something from my purse. Please return it.

FRED. What're you missing, Evelyn?

EVELYN. There is a letter inside that newspaper, and it doesn't belong to you.

FRED. Letter? From who?

EVELYN. Fred, you're angry with Toby. Not with me. Don't bring me into this.

FRED. You've been here for months. We don't know the first thing about you.

EVELYN. That is simply untrue. Don't be like this. We are all friends here.

FRED. Oh, come on. You're soft and sweet, just want everyone to be friends and do little activities. But I think it's all smoke and mirrors, Evelyn. We don't actually know anything about you. Your husband seems to know about you, though. That's why he wrote a letter supporting Natalie Clark.

CANDACE. What's going on?

FRED. Nothing. Ask Evelyn. Ask Evelyn anything. Try to get a straight answer.

(He hands **EVELYN** *the letter.)*

CANDACE. *(quietly)* What was that about?

EVELYN. Oh, you know Fred. He's such a caveman. He said some inappropriate things about unwed mothers, I disagreed, and he got all defensive.

CANDACE. What? What did he say?

EVELYN. Oh, honey, I'm sure he wasn't talking about you specifically.

CANDACE. I can't believe he'd do that.

EVELYN. You know how he can be. Just give him some space.

(The door opens. It's **ROBERTA.***)*

ROBERTA. I had another lapse!

LILA. Oh my word.

CANDACE. You didn't!

ROBERTA. It's not my fault. The stress. It got to me. Happens around the holidays. I brought six copies of Lord of the Flies, who's in?

TOBY. I'm gonna miss my chair.

ROBERTA. I brought my own, got it as far as the elevator. Go get it.

TOBY. Sure.

(**TOBY** *exits.*)

ROBERTA. Why are you all dressed alike? Are they making us wear uniforms now?

EVELYN. Christmas presents. From Lila.

ROBERTA. You look like an Osmond family portrait. Lila, have you taken up telemarketing?

LILA. Not now, dear, I'm grading portfolios.

CANDACE. We found a way for her to teach.

ROBERTA. Well, good for Lila.

CANDACE. I'm gonna go hold doors for Toby.

ROBERTA. You're in a delicate condition. Make Fred do it.

CANDACE. I'm not asking him for anything.

(*She exits.*)

ROBERTA. He's gonna bang the hell outta my chair if he's not careful. I'd better supervise. Nobody go anywhere. Ha ha ha!

(**ROBERTA** *exits.* **EVELYN** *looks at* **LILA**, *then goes to* **FRED**. *She stands over him, modeling her sweater.*)

FRED. What?

EVELYN. I'm showing you my sweater. Lila can't hear us. Just look at my sweater. Fred, I want you to pay very close attention, because I am only going to say this once. I am here for one reason – to clear my name. That is my problem, so that is my focus. Now, if you keep this shit up, you will become my problem, and you will become my focus. You do not want that.

FRED. Now we're getting someplace. The real Evelyn Reid's finally showing up.

EVELYN. And look at the craftsmanship on your neckline. May I see? (*Takes his collar in her hands, now face to face.*) If you really think I'm so clever, maybe you shouldn't be trying to make me angry, Fred. Just let me be. Back off.

FRED. You threatening me?

EVELYN. No, Fred. I consider you a friend. Please don't put me in this position.

FRED. What's that supposed to mean?

EVELYN. The problem for bullies like you is sometimes you push the wrong person too far, and then you have to deal with the consequences.

FRED. I'm guessing this is what your husband meant by "a history of duplicitous behavior."

EVELYN. About a month ago, I was repeatedly subjected to your unwelcome sexual advances.

FRED. What?

EVELYN. You sent me pornographic pictures, text messages of a sexual nature. I asked you to stop. You were so horribly persistent, all night long, until I threatened to involve the police. You called me a frigid bitch.

FRED. What the hell are you talking about?

EVELYN. I still have all the messages saved on my phone. My call history and phone bill clearly show they came from your number. Don't you remember? The next day Roberta found your phone in her purse.

FRED. Jesus Christ.

EVELYN. You already broke a kid's wrist, Fred. A sexual harassment charge would end your career. And you don't seem like a guy with a lot left to lose. Toby's right, isn't he? Not setting a place for Freddie Junior this Christmas?

FRED. Back off, Evelyn.

EVELYN. Calm down, Fred. Never show where you're weak. Someone could take advantage.

(**CANDACE** *and* **ROBERTA** *return, followed by* **TOBY**, *carrying an upholstered chair.*)

ROBERTA. Watch the door frame!

TOBY. How the hell did you get this here by yourself?

ROBERTA. I know an excellent car service. My driver's a former student.

(*The phone rings.* **CANDACE** *answers.*)

CANDACE. Metzger, 704. Thank you.

(She hangs up.)

TOBY. Is it a hearing?

CANDACE. Yeah.

ROBERTA. Well hell, I guess I didn't need the chair.

CANDACE. They're ready for you, Fred.

(FRED is caught in a single spotlight, addressed by the unseen voice.)

ATWOOD. Good afternoon, Mr. Disalvo.

FRED. Coach Disalvo, if you don't mind.

ATWOOD. Our apologies, Mr. Disalvo. Only legal titles are allowed on the record. My name is Ms. Atwood, these are my colleagues Mr. McClintock, Mrs. Aktar, and Dr. Simonovsky. We appreciate you coming in. According to your file, you were suspended from your position as a football coach and health and physical education teacher at PS 201, Eleanor Roosevelt High, Sunnyside, is that correct?

FRED. That is correct.

ATWOOD. You have been accused of using unnecessary force in disrupting an altercation between students, resulting in the injury of a minor child. The agreement with the minor child's family waives pressing criminal charges, provided satisfactory disciplinary action is taken by this committee. Mr. Disalvo, would you care to address the charge against you?

FRED. Yes. Thank you, Ms. Atwood, and the rest of you too. Look. Those minor children, as you describe them, each weigh close to two hundred pounds. One of 'em got kicked off the wrestling team for gouging his opponent's eyes, and the one who ended up with a broken wrist is repeating the tenth grade because he missed four months of school while he was in juvy. And those minor children decided, for fun, to pounce on Danny Copeland. That boy weighs a buck twenty soaking wet, barely talks above a whisper. Danny

Copeland gets hit at home, and by somebody who knows the right way to do it. Take a belt to his back, to his butt, to the back of his legs. Clothes cover it up. But I've seen him in the locker room, because he's always the last one to dress out for gym class.

Somebody has been trying to toughen that boy up, hoping he'll change, or if he won't change he'll at least stand up for himself. But boys like him just end up broken. They won't fight back.

If those two teenage thugs want somebody to fight, seems to me it oughta be somebody their own size. And in that building, I'm about the only one who fits the bill. So yeah, I used force, but it wasn't unnecessary. Somebody's gotta make them leave kids like Danny Copeland alone. They can't help it, the way they are.

If we handle this wrong, they grow up knowing that when we were in a position to defend them, we couldn't be bothered. And they will hate us, and blame us for their misery. We will have to answer why we didn't DO something, make their lives a little easier.

Look. I am a good teacher, I love what I do. I hurt that overgrown punk and I'm sorry. But Jesus, help me. We're supposed to be preparing these kids for something more than tests. We're supposed to prepare them for life, and I don't know how to help kids like… Danny Copeland…survive out there. And if they don't survive, it's on our hands. And sometimes, they don't survive. Do you understand that? Do you know what parents go through when one of these kids decides no one's on their side, and they choose not to survive?

Please, if you can sit here in judgment of me you must have some kind of answers. Help me do something that actually works, because I keep looking for an answer, and all I'm finding are the wrong ones.

(Blackout.)

End of Act One

ACT TWO

Scene One

(Two months later. It's just before Valentine's Day, and there are paper hearts strung over the door. Canvases have been hung featuring amateur paintings. EVELYN, LILA, ROBERTA, TOBY, and a very pregnant CANDACE are gathered together. ROBERTA is seated in her chair. The women all hold stacks of paper. TOBY holds his laptop computer. They are all reading aloud.)

CANDACE. "Hudson! Don't come any closer! There's a sonic force field surrounding me that will destroy your mind!"

TOBY. "Captain Logan! Are you hurt?"

CANDACE. "The force field is powered with testosterone! Our crew is being held captive in the catacombs! The Queen is using them as fuel!"

TOBY. "Our men aren't going to be batteries for these Amazon psychos!"

CANDACE. "You've got to find a way to get me down! The Queen's going to enslave me, and give me wings like the rest of them!"

TOBY. "Not on my shift, Captain."

LILA. "Foolish man, why have you come here?"

TOBY. "You! You're the women from the river!"

EVELYN. "Captain Logan belongs to The Queen now. If you attempt to rescue her, you will be captured and put to use."

LILA. "The pain you will endure is beyond human comprehension. You must go."

CANDACE. "Yes, John, just go! Save yourself!"

TOBY. "We have already lost our entire crew! Captain Logan is all I have left! We are going back to Earth!"

EVELYN. "How unfortunate that your human emotions prevent you from doing what is reasonable."

TOBY. "You had emotions once! Before you were enslaved! You both did! Please! I love her!"

EVELYN. *(dropping character)* Yes!

CANDACE. *(dropping character)* Oh, I knew it! I knew he loved her! Oh, Toby!

ROBERTA. Hush! Keep reading! When do I come back in?

TOBY. *(reading the action)* "EkanTa is unmoved. But a flicker of emotion registers in LosiRa's face. A single tear forms in her eye and rolls down her cheek. Her wings spread wide, and she grabs John, lifting him into the air, hiding him on a small ledge in the rock formation."

LILA. "Stay here, John Hudson! Be silent!"

CANDACE. "John. Whatever happens. Know that I love you too."

TOBY. "A, um, a rumble in the distance grows louder. EkanTa and LosiRa fall to the ground. A figure in the distant sky grows larger, until we see that it is the queen, flying with the speed of a comet, her black wings unfurled. She is breathtaking in her majestic terror. She descends, and lands on her feet without a sound."

ROBERTA. "Rise, slave girls. Why have you traveled so far into the Barren Lands? What service will you be to your ruler here?"

EVELYN. "Your majesty. We are EkanTa and LosiRa, guards of the eastern tower. We received a report that the man of Earth, John Hudson, might be found here, attempting to free the prisoner."

ROBERTA. "Who gave this report?"

LILA. "Oh, I forget the name. Young, blonde. Big white wings."

ROBERTA. "That would be all of you."

LILA. "Yes, your majesty, I think that's why it's so hard to remember. Perhaps if we wore name badges, like the Earth people do."

ROBERTA. "Insolence! Do you not fear your own death? I will bear down upon you with the fire of ten thousand suns! Beware the hellhounds of your monarch's curse!" *(delighted, breaks character.)* Oh, Toby. Now she talks like a queen! You read "The Oresteia."

TOBY. I took your advice.

ROBERTA. That line is pure Clytamestra. Oh, this is fabulous. "The fire of ten thousand suns." Aeschylus himself would have used that.

EVELYN. You have a flair, Toby.

LILA. I don't normally enjoy these sorts of films, but I would go to this one. If only to see the Queen's floating ice palace.

TOBY. You don't think that's too Narnia? I worried it was overkill.

CANDACE. I don't think so. It makes sense that she'd live in a floating ice castle. I buy that.

ROBERTA. She is removed from the world she rules. Cold, hard. It's all very fitting.

CANDACE. But her spy, the smoke beast? You totally ripped that off from *Lost.*

TOBY. That TV show doesn't have a monopoly on evil smoke monsters.

CANDACE. Actually, they kinda do. It'd be like putting a yellow brick road in there. That's somebody else's game.

EVELYN. What if it were a monster made of ice crystals? The slave girls would know they're being watched when it gets cold.

TOBY. That's not bad.

CANDACE. Somebody help me up. Captain Logan needs to pee.

> (**EVELYN** *helps her out of her chair.* **LILA** *pulls a binder from her knitting bag.* **CANDACE** *exits.*)

ROBERTA. Toby, can we go back to the scene just before the core explosion on Omega Seven? I made a few notes, nothing major, just a question about the timeline.

TOBY. Sure.

ROBERTA. *(getting up)* Come over here.

> *(She heads for the desk.* **TOBY** *follows.)*

LILA. You know she's angling for more lines.

EVELYN. Well that's just unfair. Ever since Roberta found her inner Faye Dunaway our parts are getting smaller and smaller.

LILA. It's alright, I read ahead. She dies in twelve pages, at the hands of her own slave girls.

EVELYN. Well, good. She deserves it.

> *(They laugh.)*

TOBY. *(to* **ROBERTA**, *looking at his laptop)* Hold on, I've got a different version of the assault on the fortress, where the Queen comes in earlier, so she knows Captain Logan isn't dead.

ROBERTA. Ooooh. I like that idea.

LILA. Look at this. From my clandestine instruction. My students have been studying Dali, and I had them create works in his style, inspired by what they see every day. This is Jerome's. He works at Burger King. Look at this detail.

EVELYN. That's amazing. And it makes me feel really terrible about our work on the walls.

LILA. He's been studying under me for several years.

EVELYN. We will too, at this rate. All the money I'm spending on a lawyer, the meetings with the union. Nothing's helping.

LILA. You'll have your chance, Evelyn. We're all in the same boat.

EVELYN. Somewhat. Oh, and now I'm not getting paid, by the way. I have direct deposit. My paycheck didn't go through on the seventh. Are they trying to make it so intolerable that we'll just quit?

LILA. Plenty of people do. Harold? The teacher who was in here before you? He got sick of waiting, now he works at a library.

EVELYN. I've got to have the hearing. I need them to put on paper that it was all untrue, or there's always going to be people wondering, you know?

ROBERTA. Damn it, Toby, you're not staying consistent with the allegory here! Is she a metaphor for the powerless role of women in society, or a commentary on abuse of influence by the underqualified? Who's your Queen? Hillary Clinton or Sarah Palin? *(Looks at* **LILA** *&* **EVELYN**.*)* Just helping Toby.

EVELYN. Of course.

LILA. So Evelyn, what are you and your husband doing for Valentine's Day? Anything special?

EVELYN. We haven't talked about it. We'll do dinner I guess.

LILA. But it's tomorrow night. You haven't made plans for tomorrow night?

EVELYN. Not yet. We're spontaneous. What about you?

LILA. Oh, we drive upstate and go hang out with some old hippies. It's delightful. Back when we were young and beautiful, we'd have a Lupercalia feast on the 14th. There wasn't anything authentic about our paganism, we just didn't want to admit we were celebrating Valentine's. Because we were so countercultural, of course. You're still young and beautiful, Evelyn. Make sure you don't pass on chances to dance around naked in the snow, because you'll be glad for the memories.

TOBY. Wait, what did I miss?

EVELYN. Lila was just telling me to dance around naked in the snow.

ROBERTA. Don't do that. And Lila, at your age you should know better.

LILA. We don't do it anymore. Now we just pass a joint and talk about it, which is what old hippies do. But we all share the same memories, so it feels like we're all doing it again.

TOBY. You're funny.

LILA. All the people at the old house, they couldn't believe it when Ezra and I wanted to be monogamous, live alone, move to the city... But that feeling of shared memories, a communal experience, we wanted to have that just between us. That's the delight of marriage, isn't it?

EVELYN. Of course.

LILA. This has to be a tough time for you two. With what that awful girl accused you of. Your husband must be pretty special, standing beside you.

EVELYN. He's a good man.

LILA. Well, take time tomorrow and make sure you let him know that.

(**CANDACE** returns.)

CANDACE. Move! Someone's coming!

ROBERTA. What?

CANDACE. There's two people from the D.O.E. doing spot checks on the rooms!

TOBY. Oh man! Go! Go! Go!

ROBERTA. Oh shit! It's the fuzz!

(A flurry of activity. **ROBERTA** tears down the Valentine hearts. **CANDACE** makes her desk presentable. **LILA** stashes her binder and grabs her knitting. **EVELYN** pulls a book of crossword puzzles from her purse, **TOBY** sits in his chair and types, and **ROBERTA** sits, reading. A long moment.)

EVELYN. This must be what Anne Frank felt like.

ROBERTA. Ugh. I never liked Anne Frank's diary. Hated teaching it

LILA. You're not allowed to say you hate Anne Frank's diary, Roberta.

ROBERTA. Why not? I daresay I wouldn't care for any book written by a pre-adolescent girl.

LILA. You say these things just to be controversial. I'm going to start recording you just so you can hear how horrible you are sometimes.

ROBERTA. It'd be a hell of a lot more interesting than that diary.

CANDACE. Will you stop? I don't want them to walk in and hear you bad-mouthing Anne Frank, for god's sake! Just sit there and be quiet!

(Everyone sits in silence.)

TOBY. Is this really what we used to do in here?

CANDACE. Shh. Toby.

EVELYN. I'm sure it's alright if we have a conversation. But I do agree we should refrain from slandering Anne Frank.

CANDACE. I don't know what they want! Just stay quiet!

TOBY. You're the proctor, you know the rules. Talking is okay.

CANDACE. I don't actually know the rules. I wasn't trained. All those rules you used to follow I just made up!

ROBERTA. You little devil!

EVELYN. When they come in, can we ask about our hearings?

ROBERTA. Yeah, that should be good for a laugh.

CANDACE. What if there's something you're supposed to be doing and nobody told me? Oh, god, this is so bad.

TOBY. I don't think they're coming.

ROBERTA. Why would they check a janitor's closet?

CANDACE. Because we're not really a janitor's closet, and they know that because this is their building! *(The phone rings.)* Oh god! We're busted!

LILA. Candace, calm down. We haven't been doing anything wrong.

CANDACE. People checking rooms, phones ringing? What is going on?

ROBERTA. Answer the phone, Candace.

CANDACE. *(Answering.)* Metzger, 704. Reid? Yes. Oh, hold on. Evelyn?

EVELYN. Yeah?

CANDACE. It's Payroll. What bank are you with?

EVELYN. Chase.

CANDACE. Chase. Okay. Evelyn, they've got you listed as Middlesex Savings Bank.

EVELYN. Well, that's not me.

CANDACE. That's not her. It's Chase.

TOBY. Middlesex Savings is in Massachusetts. My grandparents live in Bedford.

EVELYN. Wanna ask your grandmother to go pick up my paycheck? Might be more efficient.

CANDACE. Got it. *(She hangs up.)* They said to bring in a voided check tomorrow. god, that was close. I thought it was a hearing.

LILA. Candace, the hearings are a good thing. We want hearings.

ROBERTA. The hell we do.

LILA. Fine. Everybody but Roberta wants a hearing.

CANDACE. I don't want anyone to leave. I like the way things are. Maybe they will think we're a janitor's closet. Everybody stay quiet.

ROBERTA. Toby, use this experience to inform you as a dramatist. We are cowering in fear, just like astronaut John Hudson hiding from the Alien Queen.

LILA. I hope you'll use your screenwriting talents to inspire your students when you return to your classroom, dear.

CANDACE. I hope you'll use your screenwriting talents to become a screenwriter.

EVELYN. He could do both.

ROBERTA. Actually, no. He can't. Toby, you enjoy screenwriting. Do that.

TOBY. I'll be fine. I just gotta be more creative, I guess. Find a way to work around the system. I could enjoy it, eventually.

ROBERTA. Eventually. That sounds fulfilling.

TOBY. I like teaching. It's the school system I can't stand.

ROBERTA. Fred used to say that.

EVELYN. Fred used to say a lot of things.

CANDACE. You can be a Sci-Fi writer who teaches school to pay the bills until you're famous, Toby.

ROBERTA. That's not uncommon. That's what Daniel Marcos did.

LILA. Who's Daniel Marcos?

ROBERTA. Taught Algebra at my school back in the eighties, while he was trying to make it as a songwriter.

TOBY. And now he's a songwriter?

ROBERTA. No, he's dead. Died of alcohol poisoning. Alone, broken, miserable. Dreams unfulfilled. But things might be different for you, Toby. Go ahead and try to do both.

LILA. Roberta, you're hardly in a position to criticize someone for staying in a job they don't want.

ROBERTA. I'm encouraging him to be solution-minded, Lila. I wasn't happy in my classroom, so I found a solution.

TOBY. Maybe I should just go back and drop a few F-bombs on the Catholic kids.

CANDACE. No, they'd just fire you. Roberta can get away with it because everybody's afraid of mean old ladies.

ROBERTA. This is true.

CANDACE. Toby, just do what's going to make you happy.

LILA. Absolutely. Follow your dream.

EVELYN. No, Toby. Dreams are nice, but life is based on *plans*. Do what makes sense. When you have your hearing, tell them what they want to hear, and keep your job while plot your next move. Safety first.

ROBERTA. Is that what John Proctor would have done?

TOBY. No. John Proctor showed honor, and told the truth.

EVELYN. Yes, and look what happened to him. You know who turns out okay at the end of "The Crucible"? Abigail Williams. She tries to work within the system, then she tries to control it, and when it gets to be too much, she grabs some cash and gets on the next boat out of town.

ROBERTA. And you call that a happy ending?

EVELYN. She's the only one in that play who even has the potential for a happy ending, because she always has a Plan B, ready to go. Smart girl.

LILA. What an interesting take, Evelyn.

(*The phone rings.*)

CANDACE. Oh god!

ROBERTA. Stop that!

TOBY. Maybe it's payroll again.

CANDACE. (*answering*) Metzger, 704. Yes. Thank you.

(*She hangs up.*)

TOBY. Well? Is it time?

CANDACE. Yeah. For Roberta.

(*Immediately* ROBERTA *is caught in a single overhead light. All others depart. She is addressed by the unseen voice.*)

ATWOOD. Good afternoon, Mrs. Burke. My name is Ms. Atwood, these are my colleagues Mr. Stinson, Miss Rabinowitz, and Doctor O'Loughlin. We appreciate you coming in. According to your file, this is your fourth suspension from your position as an English teacher at PS 482, Paul Robeson Complex, Bronx, is that correct?

ROBERTA. Yep.

ATWOOD. Mrs. Burke, in the last two years you have been suspended for using profanities in the presence of students with alarming frequency. Do you care to explain?

ROBERTA. Yes, Ms. Atwood. In recent years I found myself unprepared for the change in attitudes of my students, as well as the shifting expectations of my own position as their instructor. I allowed my own frustration to lead to a series of unfortunate –

ATWOOD. Mrs. Burke, based upon your psychological evaluation and interviews with your colleagues, and the *consistency* of these incidents, the board has determined you are either disinterested in or incapable of maintaining a healthy learning environment. We find you are no longer fit for service in New York public schools.

ROBERTA. Look, Atwood. I might have taken this too far, but I am fully capable educating my students.

ATWOOD. I'm sorry, Mrs. Burke, the facts prove otherwise.

ROBERTA. Please. I'm three months away from retirement.

ATWOOD. You were. That is no longer the case.

ROBERTA. You can't do this! What am I supposed to do?

ATWOOD. Thank you for your time, Mrs. Burke.

(Blackout.)

Scene Two

(Seven weeks later. **TOBY** *and* **EVELYN** *are hanging baby shower decorations.)*

TOBY. Is it weird to give a shower for someone if she's giving away the baby?

EVELYN. I don't think so. People like presents, no matter the occasion.

TOBY. What'd you get her?

EVELYN. Shoes. Really great shoes. The reward for her being able to see her feet again. How about you?

TOBY. Um, an iPad.

EVELYN. Toby, that's so expensive!

TOBY. Well, that way while she's out on leave she can watch movies or chat online with, you know, whoever.

EVELYN. Very thoughtful. But, gosh, Toby. Who will she know who's available to chat in the middle of the day? Let me think...

TOBY. We're just friends, Evelyn.

EVELYN. I didn't say otherwise.

TOBY. You're smirking.

EVELYN. You're blushing.

TOBY. She's a nice person.

EVELYN. Absolutely.

TOBY. Hey, Evelyn? When your husband, um, asked you out? How'd he do it?

EVELYN. Oh, the usual way. He just came up and asked. You know. You've asked a girl out before. Haven't you?

TOBY. Of course I have. *(They continue decorating.)* It's just that no one's ever said yes. Just wanted to hear how it happens when it works.

EVELYN. Oh, Toby. *(a pause)* We worked together. We had the same lunch period, so we sat together in the cafeteria and got to know each other. Eventually he asked me out to a movie. It just sort of grew from there. You've already laid the groundwork. Candace would be crazy not to spend time with you.

TOBY. Your husband's a teacher?

EVELYN. Yes. Algebra and geometry.

TOBY. Do you still teach at the same school?

EVELYN. We did, when I was still there.

TOBY. Wow. It must be hard for you guys, with what the girl accused you of. Him still having to see her every day.

EVELYN. It was. He changed schools. He's not there anymore.

TOBY. The best thing, probably.

EVELYN. It made sense.

TOBY. Will he go back when you do?

EVELYN. *(picking up tape dispenser)* We'll see. He really likes the new job.

TOBY. Is he gonna –

EVELYN. We're out of tape. There's no one in the room next door yet. Will you go steal theirs?

TOBY. Oh, sure.

> *(**TOBY** exits. **EVELYN** sits. For an instant, her face betrays her, and then she recovers remarkably quickly. **LILA** enters with a pastry box.)*

LILA. Good morning.

EVELYN. Hey! Got the cupcakes?

LILA. I did. And I thought of the best gift! Other than the blanket, which is really for the baby. I got Candace a salon appointment for a manicure and a pedicure. All the things you can't do when you're pregnant.

> *(**TOBY** returns, with a tape dispenser.)*

TOBY. Got it! Morning Lila.

LILA. Morning Toby. You look nice.

TOBY. Well, you know, a party and all. Evelyn, wanna get these streamers up?

> *(**ROBERTA** enters, with a gift in hand.)*

ROBERTA. Ah. It's good to be home.

LILA. Roberta, dear, I'm so glad you came.

(**LILA** *hugs* **ROBERTA***, which causes her to stiffen, because that's just how she is.*)

ROBERTA. Well what else do I have to do with my day? I can't believe I had to get here so gee dee early for Candace. So, no more hearings, obviously.

EVELYN. Not since yours. What'd you get her?

ROBERTA. *(sitting in her chair)* A neck massager.

LILA. How lovely. And only mildly inappropriate.

ROBERTA. It'll keep her outta trouble. When used properly.

TOBY. I don't get it.

EVELYN. You don't want the explanation. Especially from Roberta.

(**CANDACE** *walks in with some effort. She is shockingly pregnant.*)

ROBERTA. Shit!

CANDACE. What? Roberta?

LILA. Oh, oh no!

TOBY. Why are you here so early?

EVELYN. Surprise!

CANDACE. What?

LILA. It's a party!

TOBY. Ta-da!

CANDACE. Party for what?

ROBERTA. It's a baby shower. Before your tenant moves out.

EVELYN. Surprise!

CANDACE. But…oh my god. You guys! And Roberta came! To a party for me! *(She begins to cry.)* Oh my god I love you all so much! And there's cupcakes!

LILA. Oh, sweetie.

(*She takes* **CANDACE***'s arm and leads her to* **ROBERTA***.* **ROBERTA** *stares at her.*)

ROBERTA. What?

LILA. Get up. That's the comfy chair.

ROBERTA. Yes, that's why I brought it here.

EVELYN. It always comes back to the chairs.

CANDACE. It's fine. Just bring me my chair.

(TOBY brings her the desk chair, and she sits.)

ROBERTA. So, Candace. How much longer?

CANDACE. Well, Friday's my last day, and then it's just, oh, any time.

ROBERTA. Have you found a home for it yet?

LILA. It's a baby, not a puppy, Roberta.

ROBERTA. Same principle, similar process. I had to do two interviews to get my last cat.

TOBY. She found a cool couple. We all looked at the finalists' applications together.

LILA. They all seemed like such nice people.

ROBERTA. Well I hope you were creative and went with gays or something.

CANDACE. Their names are Tim and Allison. He works in drywall –

EVELYN. Which pays much better than you'd think.

CANDACE. And Allison's co-owner of a cupcake bakery in Williamsburg. They're going to put a nursery in the back, so she can bring the baby to the bakery. Isn't that sweet?

TOBY. Candace gets free cupcakes for life.

ROBERTA. You traded that baby for cupcakes.

CANDACE. Allison's also a cancer survivor. She had a hysterectomy at twenty-six. A lot of agencies won't take them, because, well you know.

ROBERTA. The cancer might come back.

CANDACE. But I thought about what you said. Perfectly healthy people get cancer *after* they have kids. And she already fought it once and won. Who's to say she wouldn't survive again if it came back? I just felt like I was their best shot, you know? They want a kid real bad.

ROBERTA. *(standing slowly)* Alright. You can have the comfy chair.

CANDACE. Really?

ROBERTA. Oh, just take the gee dee chair and don't talk to me for a second.

> (**ROBERTA** *goes to the door, with her back to the room.* **CANDACE** *rises, and* **TOBY** *helps her sit in the comfy chair.*)

CANDACE. I didn't mean to upset her.

LILA. You didn't upset her. She's experiencing gratitude and she doesn't know what to do with it.

EVELYN. Just let her go through it. It's all very new and confusing.

TOBY. Candace, ya want a cupcake?

CANDACE. Oh, yes please.

LILA. Ooh! I have news. I got an email from another one of my seniors last night. She got into Cal Arts.

TOBY. Ha! Don't you know this is driving your principal nuts?

LILA. It's a mixed blessing, really. Now they'll think they don't need me, if they even keep the program. I may have instructed my way right out of a job. But it's great for my kids. I hear Saint Andrew's is hiring, though.

EVELYN. You should go for it, Lila. They'd be lucky to have you.

LILA. It would be nice to teach again, without hiding in a corner on Toby's laptop.

ROBERTA. You will apply. Face it, Lila, you're a lifer. You'll never retire. A room full of adoring students is essential to your survival. Which is just so bizarre.

TOBY. And she's back.

LILA. What about you, Roberta? You getting by okay?

ROBERTA. Never better. I had my savings, and one of my former students is a doctor. She diagnosed me with dementia, so now I can file for wrongful termination due to disability.

LILA. Roberta, you do not have dementia. You're frighteningly aware.

ROBERTA. Oh, who can really say for sure? If you look at yourself closely for long enough, you can find a nice pocket of crazy. Toby, is my screenplay done?

TOBY. I brought you a copy. I'm in a writer's workshop on Tuesday nights.

CANDACE. It's so great! Like, blockbuster James Cameron movie great.

ROBERTA. Evelyn, that lawyer you can't afford doing you any good yet?

EVELYN. He's trying. Everybody's trying.

TOBY. Evelyn had to see the shrink!

ROBERTA. Oh, you should've called me. I've been in there a dozen times. Made him cry once.

EVELYN. And Natalie Clark, my favorite student? She had to be evaluated, too. I could have gone in quacking like a duck and I'd still seem more reliable than her. I feel great about my hearing, if I could ever have the damn thing.

CANDACE. I'd be sad if I came back and you weren't here.

TOBY. Any of us could be gone.

EVELYN. Toby's right. Any of us could get a hearing. Or Lila could get that job.

TOBY. No, it's…not that. *I* got a job. The Natural History Museum was hiring tour guides, so I figured what the hell, ya know? And I got it. It'll be like teaching, without the school crap. Evelyn was right. I needed a Plan B.

LILA. Oh, Toby, that's wonderful.

CANDACE. You're leaving? How long have you known?

TOBY. Last Wednesday. But I don't start 'til the fifteenth, so I figured I'd stick around here, collect another check.

ROBERTA. I taught you well.

TOBY. And without papers to grade or anything, I can write in my off time.

EVELYN. We'll miss you, Toby.

CANDACE. Yeah. We will.

TOBY. I'll miss you too.

ROBERTA. Oh, this is getting ridiculous. You two are like a Jane Austen novel. One of the lesser works.

TOBY. Um, guys? Could I have a minute alone with Candace?

EVELYN. Of course.

ROBERTA. Alone? Where are we supposed to go?

LILA. Everyone, come look at the cupcakes.

> (**LILA**, **EVELYN**, *and* **ROBERTA** *go to the desk, then listen intently.*)

TOBY. Candace. I, um, what I mean is –

> *(The phone rings.)*

EVELYN. Oh come on! He's so close!

CANDACE. I have to get that. I forgot to call in my absentee report.

TOBY. Sure. I mean, yeah.

> *(He helps her stand, and she makes her way to the desk for the phone.)*

CANDACE. Metzger, 704. Sorry. I've got Wadkins, Lila and Burke, Roberta – I mean, no! I don't have her! Whaaaaat? Ha ha! I meant Reid, Evelyn and... Oh. Yeah. Okay. *(She hangs up.)* Toby. Guess who's first hearing of the day? You don't have to go if you don't wanna.

TOBY. Yeah, that's true. I guess I can just go home.

LILA. Toby Fleming, if you don't go to that hearing, I'll never forgive you.

TOBY. Why?

LILA. Because you're the only one of us who isn't going in on bended knee, begging for your job. Now damn it, you get in there for the rest of us, and by god, you *say something*

TOBY. Okay. Okay, Lila. I can do that.

ROBERTA. Atta boy.

> (**TOBY** *takes his backpack, and removes his painting from the wall.*)

TOBY. Alright, I'm going in. I'll miss you guys.

EVELYN. You're gonna do great. Make us proud, Toby.

TOBY. Oh, Lila's students. She needs a –

EVELYN. Lila can use my laptop, it's fine.

LILA. We'll see you at the opening of your movie. I expect tickets.

ROBERTA. I expect to be cast.

> (*He stops at* **CANDACE**.)

TOBY. Candace.

CANDACE. Yes, Toby?

TOBY. I think I'm a little bit in love with you.

CANDACE. That's good. I think that's really good.

TOBY. Maybe more than a little.

CANDACE. That's even better.

TOBY. You, um, wanna go out sometime?

CANDACE. Yes. I mean, I gotta have this baby, but after that I'm totally free.

TOBY. Great.

CANDACE. Unless you wanna, you know, come to that. The baby thing. It'll take a while, and it'd be nice to have – I thought my sister might – but she's, um, a really terrible person. So I could use the company. I'm pretty sure there'll be cupcakes.

TOBY. That sounds awesome. That'd be the coolest first date ever.

ROBERTA. Jesus, they're made for each other.

CANDACE. Well, um, have a good hearing, Toby. Go kick ass.

(She kisses him.)

EVELYN. That committee won't wait.

ROBERTA. You're a writer, Toby. Use your words.

TOBY. Okay. I'm ready.

> *(Overhead light on* **TOBY**. *All others depart.* **TOBY** *is addressed by the unseen voice.)*

ATWOOD. Good morning, Mr. Fleming. My name is Ms. Atwood, these are my colleagues Mr. Bhandari, Doctor Chalmont, and Mrs. Fothergill-Moreno. We appreciate you coming in. According to your file, you were suspended from your position as a Science teacher at PS 271, Yonkers, following a classroom outburst that resulted in destruction of school property, is that correct?

TOBY. Sounds about right, Ms. Atwood.

ATWOOD. Would you care to explain your actions?

TOBY. Explain them? Huh. Nah. That's okay. Thanks, though. See, Ms. Atwood, Mr. Bhandari, Doctor Whatever, Mrs. Awkward Hyphenated Name, I don't see any point in defending my actions to people whose opinions don't matter to me. None of you are qualified to tell me if I belong in a classroom, because you don't have the balls to get in there and do it. You have no concept –

You assign ratings and guidelines like they actually mean something, and you sit at a folding table in a little room, content with authority you never earned and plausible deniability. After all, you didn't put this system in place, it was the mayor, it was the unions, it was government announcing no child would be left behind. Bullshit. You did it with your votes. You did it when you got the new guidelines and didn't take to the streets in protest. You did it when you let them cut the arts, and music, and independent thought from our classrooms. What the hell do we pay you people for?

Your system is broken. It's failing the teachers and the students. Shame on you. Shame on all of you. Fix it. This is why I'm gonna write sci-fi movies, so I can still inspire imaginations and a love for science without people like you getting in the way.

Which is a shame, really, because when you lose the people who are as pissed off as I am, nothing's gonna change! Who's gonna fight to save these kids from idiots like you? If you really cared about these kids' futures, you'd send me back to my classroom, and let me do my job.

> *(Silence hangs in the air.* **TOBY** *grows a little queasy.)*

ATWOOD. So don't quit.

TOBY. I'm sorry?

ATWOOD. Stay. Save them. From "idiots like us." Or leave, and lose any right to criticize. It's your choice, Mr. Fleming. Where do you belong?

TOBY. I belong in my classroom.

ATWOOD. Good. Welcome back.

> *(Blackout.)*

Scene Three

(Three weeks later. The decorations are gone. **EVELYN** *is curled up in the comfy chair, reading a book.* **LILA** *enters.)*

LILA. Any calls?

EVELYN. Oh, you're funny. How did it go?

LILA. I was the oldest one there.

EVELYN. You were the most experienced one there.

LILA. You know what amazed me? The smell. Public schools smell like urinal cakes, but one grows accustomed to it with time. But Saint Andrew's smelled like old books and saddle soap. It was extraordinary.

EVELYN. Oh, Lila. You'd be so happy there.

LILA. Let's not get ahead of ourselves. There were plenty of applicants. But my god, it'd be so nice to teach again.

EVELYN. Of course.

LILA. Candace called my cell, to ask how the interview went.

EVELYN. How is Candace?

LILA. She's home, resting. Says she's alright, a little sad, but alright. She'll be coming back next week.

EVELYN. Think we can keep up the charade until then?

LILA. Excuse me?

EVELYN. Playing pretend proctor.

LILA. Oh. Of course. Toby's been sleeping on her sofa. Says it's closer to his school. They're watching *Breaking Bad* together.

EVELYN. Oh, god, she should really get cable before she gets herself into trouble again.

LILA. By the way, Elena sends her regards.

EVELYN. Elena?

LILA. Mrs. Vargas. The guidance counselor at your school. I used to work with her, remember?

EVELYN. I didn't know you'd talked to her.

*(**LILA** sits, searches for her knitting in the tote bag.)*

LILA. I had the bright idea to use her as a reference. She owed me one.

EVELYN. Elena's so thoughtful. I'm sure she gave you a great recommendation.

LILA. She said your students are doing well.

EVELYN. That's a great relief.

LILA. They miss you. And your husband.

EVELYN. I'm sure they do. He's a good teacher.

LILA. That's what Elena said. One of the most popular instructors. Before he left. Elena was a reference for him as well.

EVELYN. Wow. Elena's a great reference for everyone, isn't she?

LILA. Said she hasn't spoken with him since January, when he moved to Massachusetts.

EVELYN. You can let her know he's doing very well.

LILA. You're telling me he couldn't find a teaching position in New York?

EVELYN. No, Lila. I'm not telling you anything. Elena is telling you things, because she is apparently much more interested in talking about my life than I am.

LILA. You and whatever may have happened in your marriage is not Elena's concern, and it certainly isn't mine.

EVELYN. Thank you.

LILA. Students, however…are another matter altogether. She told me about Natalie Clark. Word got out about what she accused you of, and everyone believed she lied.

EVELYN. As Roberta said, there's nothing more dangerous than a child who lies.

LILA. I couldn't agree more. But Natalie has been in Elena's office, all year, of her own accord. Begging to be believed.

EVELYN. If you tell a lie often enough, you can convince yourself it's the truth.

LILA. Oh my, yes. But the truth always comes out, doesn't it? I'm glad Elena's established some kind of dialogue with her. Those types only become more suspicious of authority with time. A teacher has a responsibility to be an advocate, especially for the kids nobody wants to listen to.

EVELYN. Actually, Lila, a teacher's responsibility is to inspire a love of your subject matter. That's the job. You seem to have forgotten that. At the end of the year, my students love history. Your students love you. That's why mine did just fine without me, and yours can't get by without you sneaking in and coaching them. You interfere to the point of distraction. I don't mean to be harsh, but you might want to think about that before you go back to a classroom.

LILA. Interesting point.

(The phone rings.)

EVELYN. *(answers, as* **CANDACE***)* Metzger, 704. Yeah. Okay. Sure. *(She hangs up.)* My god. It's time for my hearing.

LILA. I know.

EVELYN. I can't believe it. Wait, why would you know?

LILA. I'll be speaking at your hearing.

EVELYN. Really. That's unusual.

LILA. Elena gave me the opportunity to speak directly with Natalie Clark. She is a very troubled girl. But, well, my mother used to say she could smell a lie on our breath, like it was liquor. And I didn't smell a lie.

EVELYN. And you believe your infallible nose for the truth qualifies you to speak at my hearing?

LILA. I've had students like you, Evelyn. Overachieving girls from bad homes. You built yourself a good life, your instinct is to maintain it, and you'll fight dirty to do it. I understand that. But you can't do that at the expense of a child.

EVELYN. I had teachers like you, Lila. Meddling busybodies who pass judgment on everyone under the guise of being magnanimous. You have no right to interfere. You are not involved in any of this. Please, Lila. I don't want to fight you. Look. Not every one of your kids who wanted to get into a great arts program managed to do it. Do you consider those kids a failure?

LILA. No. Because my investment in each student was the same.

EVELYN. Still, you don't say, "some of my kids go to Pratt and Parsons, and some wind up doing nothing with their lives." You focus on the successes, and recognize that some students are simply beyond your help. Cut your losses. Natalie Clark is a habitual liar, and she's dealing with the consequences of that.

LILA. Except. In this instance, she's telling the truth.

EVELYN. She's a liar, Lila! I've got a stack of letters from people who back that up. Her own mother says she's a liar, and I don't deserve this!

LILA. But Evelyn. This time, she's not lying.

EVELYN. How is it fair to watch my life fall apart over a piece of trash like Natalie Clark? She gains nothing, and I lose everything!

LILA. Because she's telling the truth! And if she isn't supported when she tells the truth, she'll never see the point in doing it again. It's our job. She isn't a lost cause.

EVELYN. As far as I'm concerned, she is. I just want to get past this and try to put my life back together.

LILA. Evelyn. I am so sorry. You don't get to do that.

EVELYN. You don't want to do this, Lila. If I have to fight you, I will win.

LILA. Oh, I'm sure you have a backup plan for me too. Anyone who thinks Abigail Williams is the hero of *The Crucible* is bound to have no shortage of machinations at her disposal. Look at what you tried to do to Fred.

EVELYN. Of course you've been talking to Fred.

LILA. I emailed him to invite him to Candace's baby shower. I didn't have his number. Apparently *you* did.

EVELYN. You don't actually believe I did that, do you? With the messages? Lila, I made that up on the spot to scare him. I had to shake him up so he'd mind his own business. My god, you should know me better than that.

LILA. I agree. I should. Fred's doing well, by the way. He took an anti-bullying workshop as part of his agreement to return to school, and now he's one of the instructors.

EVELYN. Good for him.

LILA. Atonement is a powerful thing. Fred has come so far. He came to terms with the truth about his son. He tried to force a lie all those years, and the only message his son received was that he was somehow fundamentally flawed. Because he was being raised by a man obsessed with turning a lie into the truth. That's no way to live. Fred lost a son. How much are you willing to lose?

EVELYN. I don't know, Lila. You seem to think you're in a position to decide how much I lose.

LILA. I just want you to take responsibility for the choicehs you've made.

EVELYN. I do. I own every choice I've made, but I'll be damned if I roll over and give up because of this. You have no right to do this. Roberta screws the system from every angle, you celebrate it. We sneak around so Candace gets paid maternity leave, that's fine. We pretend we're in a janitor's closet, you leave the sign up. Why doesn't your precious moral compass go haywire on any of that?

LILA. Because none of that is hurting anyone.

EVELYN. That is not your call to make, you hypocritical bitch! You know what? I didn't do anything. Not one thing. I don't have to go on the defensive. They have the burden of proof.

LILA. And they have me. We'll leave it up to them to sort out what's true. But I will not be silenced, no matter what you try to make up about me.

EVELYN. Lila. Come on. I don't have to make anything up about you. You have no credibility. You have a recorded history of insubordination. And you've had contact with your students for the last five months. It's all saved on my laptop. Then tracking down my students, coercing them into your version of the truth. That's sketchy behavior from a woman who I'm fairly certain would fail a drug test. You'll lose your job, and your teaching certificate. No Saint Andrews and saddle soap smell for you. I really like you, Lila. You're a well-intentioned person. But face the facts. I would rebuild in a new career. I'm likeable, I'm clever. I'm still young enough to dance in the snow.

LILA. You certainly are clever.

EVELYN. You are too old to start over. Think of your husband. You'll lose your pension, and Ezra will have to work to support you until the day he dies. Or you'll become a burden on your girls. Does your family deserve that? The system is a disaster anyway. A few years from now, you can retire, celebrate your successes, and know you did the best you could. Or if you really think it's worth it, you can walk in there and blow up your own life just to keep me out of my classroom, and support an undeserving lost cause. *(She picks up her briefcase.)* I wish you well. I know you don't believe that, but I do. You're a smart woman, Lila. You'll do what's best.

(**EVELYN** *exits.* **LILA** *makes a decision.*)

End of Play

Lightning Source UK Ltd.
Milton Keynes UK
UKOW06f1315240716

279070UK00007B/44/P